I0784055

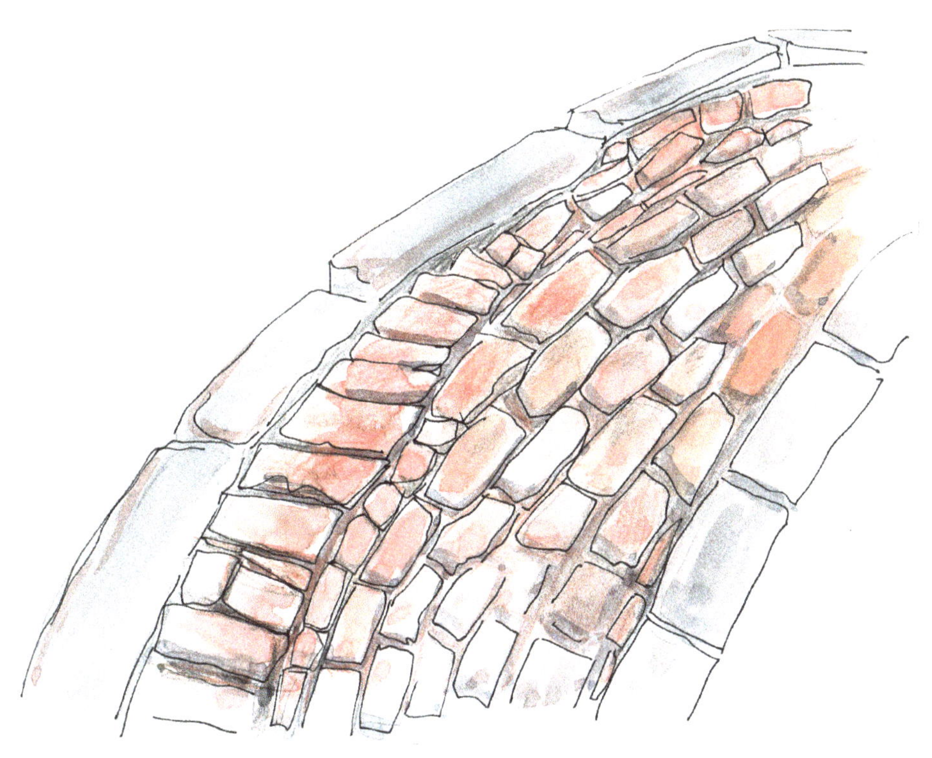

A Small City by the Sea

AN ARTIST'S VIEW OF **PORTSMOUTH**, NEW HAMPSHIRE

Sue Anne Bottomley

All rights reserved. Published by Piscataqua Press, an imprint of RiverRun Bookstore, Inc.
Printed in the United States.

Book design by Karin Tracy

Acknowledgements

I wish to acknowledge and thank those people who helped so much to make this book that is in your hands.

My family and my friends encouraged me. They said, "What are you working on now?" And "Can't wait to see it."

Our older daughter Karin was the book designer. My husband Bruce was my tech support and one of my editors. Thank you both so much. My sister Aimée and her husband Steve took over the very important job of proofreading.

Thanks to the residents of Portsmouth (whom I met while walking the streets with my sketchbook) who were curious about my project and sharing of helpful tips. I met many artists with brushes in their hands and paint on their clothes. We all shared a love of the city, the streets, the buildings, the boats, and the water.

Dedication

I dedicate this book to the residents of Portsmouth, both
to the current ones and to the memories of those long
gone. To the memory of architects, laborers, shipbuilders,
sailors, and shopkeepers. To women who birthed and raised
children. In praise of urban planners and redesigners.
In awe of public discussions and stubborn visionaries.

Introduction

This is my third book. The first one, *Colorful Journey: An Artist's Adventure Drawing Every Town in New Hampshire*, covered the entire state. One drawing for each of the 234 towns. The second one, *Pep Talks for the Would-Be, Should-Be, Artist*, is motivational in nature. It took me months of pondering before I decided to write, or draw, this new book about one small city. I am a native of the state, but I live 90 minutes inland, towards Vermont. So I am not quite a local, but certainly not a tourist either. I am a frequent visitor with perhaps fresh eyes and a deep appreciation of the place.

My plan was to produce 100 drawings/paintings done on site, on the streets of Portsmouth, over the course of one year. (I call them drawings because they are linear in nature even though they have paint on them.) So the seasons do show themselves in the drawings.

I drew in all four seasons unless it was raining or below freezing. I carried a small sketchbook, a pencil or pen, and sometimes a watercolor palette.

The many artists I met on location were friendly and sharing of other good views of the buildings, boats, and water. Street musicians, shop owners, and wait-staff were all encouraging of my project. My publisher Tom Holbrook of RiverRun Bookstore liked my idea from the start, so that gave me energy to begin, continue, and finish my grand plan.

Why Portsmouth? I like the urban feel of the small brick central core. The open Market Square is a delight in all seasons, as are the smaller winding streets that lead down to the waterfront. My sketchbook filled up with whole street scenes, as well as close up details that required me to stop and stare and look up. Other people stopped and looked up as I drew.

The South End, just a few blocks past Strawbery Banke, has a more village atmosphere. The buildings are smaller, mostly domestic in scale. And brightly colored. I counted two shops, a kayak rental, and a seafood restaurant. One could settle in and never leave.

My watch words for this book are: slow down, look up, look down, look around, become intrigued and pleased to be in the small city by the sea, Portsmouth.

A few notes about Portsmouth, New Hampshire

- 16 square miles, population about 20,000
- situated on the tidal Piscataqua River, a deep, natural harbor that is ice free year round
- fishing, lumber, and shipbuilding were the earliest trades
- home of Abenaki tribes
- **1623** first English settlers
- **1679** capital of the Royal Colony
- **1690** first warship built in North America, HMS Falkland
- **1774** Royal Colonial Capital moved inland to Exeter
- **1776** an independent government formed, six months prior to the Declaration of Independence

- **1800** the Portsmouth Naval Shipyard established in Kittery, Maine
- **1807** port closed in lead up to the War of 1812, which caused economic hardship
- **1802**, **1806**, **1813**, devastating fires, loss of hundreds of homes and buildings
- **1814** the Brick Act passed, requiring new buildings to be of brick and slate
- **1870-1900** major East Coast center for breweries
- **1950s-1970s** urban renewal featuring demolition of early buildings
- **1970s- to present**, city preservation and renovation of historic homes and buildings, encouraging tourism

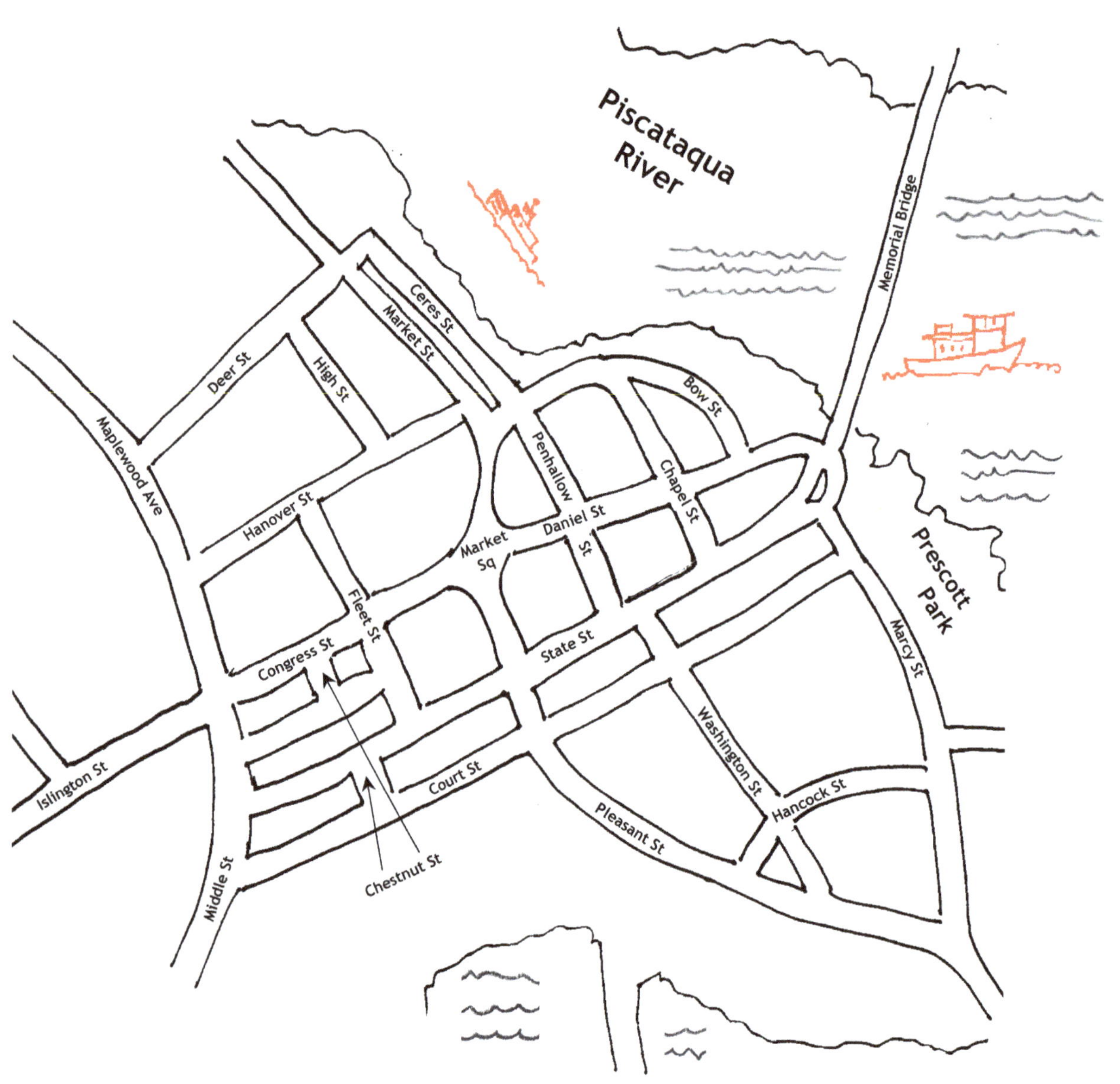

Market Square area

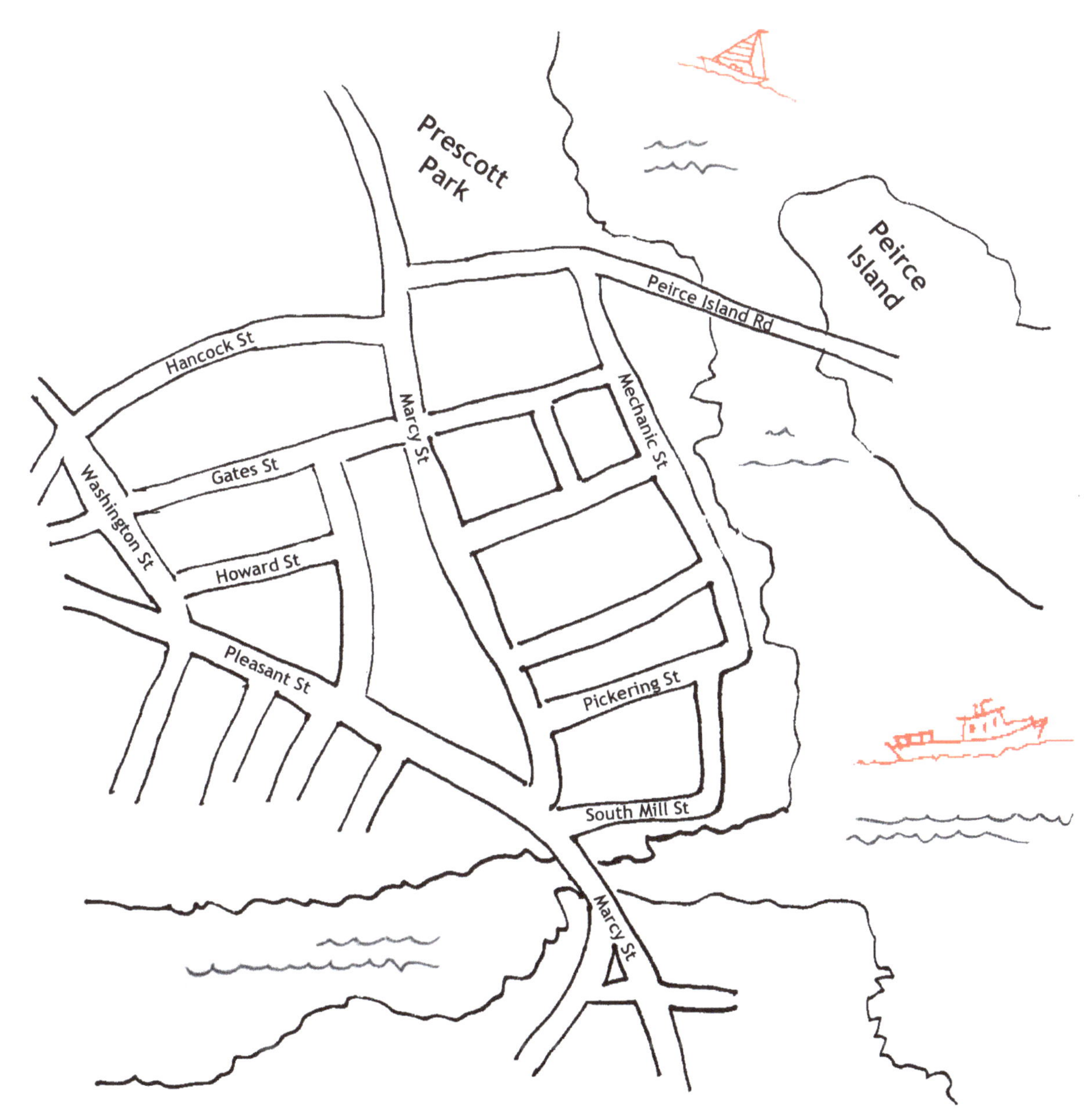

The South End

This neoclassical doorway is at the Athenaeum on Market Square.
Built in 1805, it is a membership library and gallery. Athena is
the Greek goddess of wisdom. I like to imagine it being designed
and constructed, and the curved glass panels being set into the
window frames.

The information kiosk in Market Square is almost always open, and staffed with helpful people. The busy coffee shop Breaking New Grounds sits right next to it.

This curved building forms one side of Market Square. The tall chimneys make a strong skyline. On this particular Saturday in June, the square was filled with throngs attending the annual Market Square Day.

I picked out a good spot to draw the musicians in front of the North Church in Market Square. Live music is an important part of Market Square Day, and it adds so much to the festive atmosphere.

On Market Street, just off the square, several talented street musicians entertain the passers-by. Here Bob is expertly playing the national instrument of Sweden, the nyckelharpa.

I drew the entire façade of the Athenaeum in early spring.
The proportions are grand and impressive.

The central core of Portsmouth had several fires, 1802, 1806, and
1813, which destroyed many of the earliest wooden buildings.
A law was then passed requiring all buildings in the downtown to
be of brick. This building was constructed in 1813.

The building with the curved brick wall, which I love so much, was the original Custom House from 1817 to 1860. The curved shape is repeated in the windows, the fans, and the side doorway.

At the corner of Market and Bow, the street curves and slopes down towards the Piscataqua River. The windows and sidewalk are trimmed in New Hampshire granite.

Brightly colored storefronts slow your feet down on Market Street.
The blue and yellow play off nicely against the brick and granite.

These tall warehouse buildings on Market Street were built in 1803, after a fire in 1802 destroyed the original wooden ones. The river waterfront is directly behind them.

A fine old door with a granite step, a planter, and clothing with sale prices. It is nearly impossible for me to walk quickly down Market Street.

From its source at the confluence of the Salmon Falls River, the Cocheco River, and Great Bay, the tidal Piscataqua River runs 12 miles to the open sea. Portsmouth lies at its midpoint.

The Moran tugboats are easily seen and drawn from a waterfront restaurant.

Drawn at the end of Ceres Street, elements of the working harbor are on the left, while tourists are enjoying the view from the restaurants on the right. The Memorial Bridge, a drawbridge, is in the center. The yellow cranes are at the Portsmouth Naval Shipyard, on an island in Maine.

The row of red lanterns stopped my feet on quiet Penhallow Street.
They contrast nicely with the bright blue awning on Bow Street.

Looking to my right after drawing the lanterns, this row of close up cars partially blocks the view of the Sarah Mildred Long Bridge.

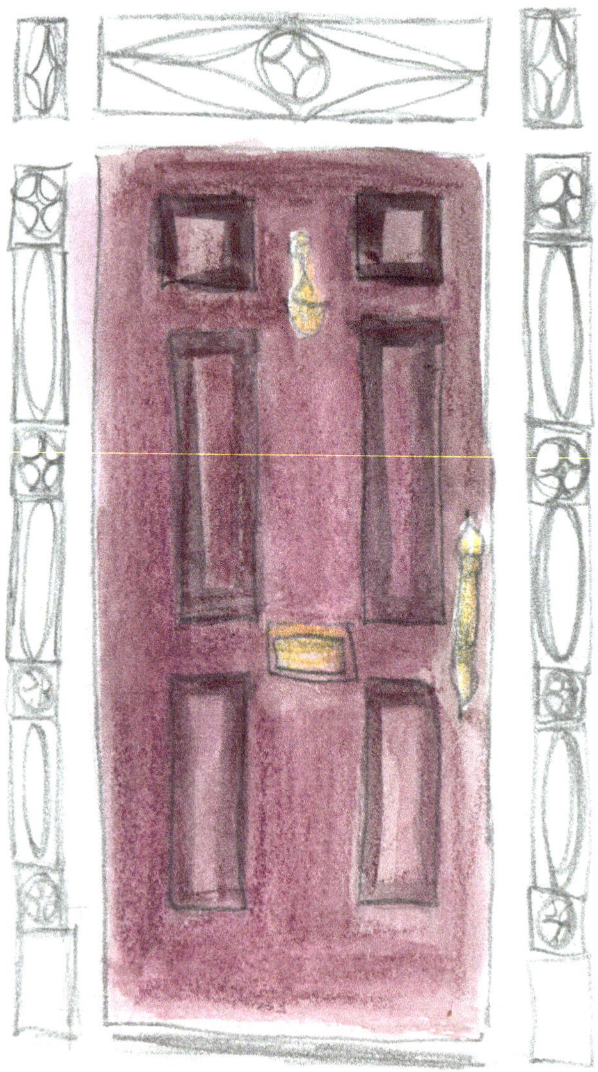

As I stood in front of this door on Pleasant Street, I envisioned the draftsman at the drawing board sketching out the shapes of the leaded glass panels and the door too. We are surrounded by the creative efforts of people long gone, but remembered by their designs.

The plant forms on the wrought iron gate on Pleasant Street are appealing. My artistic license allowed me to add the reds and blues.

Looking through the door of the Book And Bar onto State Street yielded this double image. On the left is a typical brick commercial building, while a glance to the right shows a peek of the grey granite South Church.

The wrought iron arched gate on State Street leads to the steps
of the granite South Church, built in 1826. Home to a Unitarian-
Universalist congregation, members are thought to have been
active in the Underground Railway just before the Civil War.

If you stand very close to the fence and look up to the dormer windows, this is your view of the John Langdon House on Pleasant Street. Langdon was a prominent citizen, shipbuilder, revolutionary, and elected politician.

Focusing on details is good exercise for eyes and mind. Next,
the variations in the details become apparent and fascinating.
And you can get a lot of other people on the sidewalk to look
up too. The windows are on Pleasant Street and Congress Street.

This oversized eagle above the door on Pleasant Street is carved wood, and is clutching a Stars and Stripes shield in its talons. An antiques dealer I met called it a Bellamy Eagle, after the man who carved many a similar sculpture. The leaded glass above the door is designed into the shapes of feathers.

This bronze eagle sits at the entrance to the Memorial Bridge, which spans the Piscataqua River in the heart of the city. The drawbridge is dedicated to the memory of World War I veterans.

All of these very graphic signs hang out over the street to catch your attention. Two of them are three-dimensional sculptures. They can be found on Market Street, Pleasant Street, and Commercial Alley.

Four of these are flat storefront signs, and one is a very beautiful,
sturdy piece of iron support for the shops on Ceres Street.
The signs are on Daniel Street, Fleet Street, Hanover Street,
and Mechanic Street.

The doorway to the florist on Market Street caught my eye with its arch constructed of birch boughs. I remember the sidewalk crowds that day. I just drew between the people.

And the door to the Ceres Bakery is surrounded by ivy. A very popular local eatery on Penhallow Street. By noon the chairs in the sun are filled.

Deer Street is the upper edge of The Hill, a grouping of 14 houses saved in the 1960s from demolition. The warm and cool colors caught my eye. The contrast between the ornate façade and the very plain side and back views appealed to me too.

This warm, peach painted private residence on Marcy Street has been moved twice. A newspaper, *The Oracle Of The Day*, was published in the house in 1793. And it is now called the Oracle House.

I caught a glimpse of the steeple of St. John's Church on Chapel Street as I made my way up Bow Street. The original structure, called Queen's Chapel, was built in 1638. This one was constructed in 1807 to replace one lost in the 1806 fire. The yellow and green colors can be seen from quite a distance.

While walking along Daniel Street, turn your head uphill at the corner of Chapel Street. It is another flashing glimpse of lovely old St. John's Church from the other side.

The salt mountain, as I call it, rises at the lower end of Market Street. The salt from Chile is used on the roads in the icy winter months. Beach roses grow near the long brick wall. Right next door, along the river, is the spot to embark on harbor cruises or on boat trips to the Isles of Shoals

Since the subject of boats arose on the previous page, it is time to put in this sweet little blue boat which is moored in the South End.

Looking west from the top of Portsmouth's only parking garage,
a canopy of tall trees hides blocks of houses under the branches.
A slender pink and grey church rises above the trees. The church is
called the Pearl, and it is on Pearl Street. Built in 1857, the steeple
was added in 1866. The Reverend Martin Luther King, Jr. preached
here in 1952.

Looking north from the garage, I liked the look of High Street. The houses were colorful, with varied roof lines. And I got a chance to draw the Piscataqua Bridge out on Route 95.

On a major building on Congress Street, a salamander is carved into the yellow stone. With the added foliage, the circle design becomes a square. Who carved it and why? Having a history of stone masons in my family, I like to imagine this bas-relief sculpture as it was worked on. It would have required a ladder.

Across the street from the salamander stand these three small, attached buildings with shop fronts in each, and doorways to upstairs apartments. The one on the right is probably from the 1930s. The other two are much older. Although not as harmonious as other streets, a slow walk down Congress Street, especially popping into the small shops, galleries, and restaurants, is a treat.

Unusual for the city, the Music Hall is yellow brick with some salmon paint too, to contrast nicely with the dark green trim. On this day, at this time of day, I was able to see a reflection of the red brick building across the narrow street. This ornate 900 seat theater was built in 1878. In times past, stage acts as diverse as Mark Twain and Buffalo Bill Cody have entertained the crowds here.

Looking up Chestnut Street, the eye picks up the salmon colored brick of the Music Hall. This Victorian theater has been restored, and is a vibrant part of Portsmouth's cultural life. This drawing is from 2015, two years earlier than the other. It shows a different angle, lighting, and general effect.

From a vantage point across Pleasant Street, I got in the corner of the grey granite Custom House, and the pure white wooden steeple of the North Church, which has become the symbol of Portsmouth.

This is the back view of a grand house on State Street as seen from Chestnut Street. The large areas with no windows focus your attention on the roofline with the unusually tall brick chimneys.

One of the boarders in this sea captain's house on State Street was naval hero John Paul Jones. His ships *Ranger* and *America* were built along the banks of the Piscataqua River. I included the charming herb garden and sundial in the foreground.

At the corner of Islington Street and Maplewood Avenue sits this turreted house, a private residence. The colors of buttery yellow and wine red trim are lively and eye-catching. Turrets were fashionable for many decades and may be making a comeback.

The African Burial Memorial Park on Chestnut street off of State Street is a must-see to fully appreciate the city, both its history and current day efforts to expand awareness of the slave trade in the northern states.

Tiles on the fence that surround the burial vault were made by local school children. The fence slats are shaped like boat oars, with a kente cloth motif. Flat figures represent today's residents.

This symbol, found in more than one area of the African Burial Ground, is called a sankofa. Its meaning in West Africa is reverence for the past. As well as guidance to learn from the past in order to move forward.

While hoping not to trip on cobblestones and uneven pavement, my favorite way of walking down a street is to look up to see where and how the building roofline meets the sky. The Rockingham Hotel is a marvel of ambitious design plus skilled brick masonry on State Street.

The white wooden building attached to the Middle Street Baptist Church has wonderful finials on top of the central turret. It requires a bit of squinting and neck craning to take them in.

I stopped and drew these three finials on two streets, Pleasant Street and Market Street. They are white painted wood and all at eye level. It is entertaining to compare and contrast these decorative features. Perhaps they were all turned on the same lathe by one expert woodworker.

The fast moving Piscataqua is a tidal river that connects the Portsmouth harbor with the open sea. One bright, breezy, blue sky day, we took a small boat, the Challenger, out to the Isles of Shoals. These nine islands, shared by New Hampshire and Maine, are about six miles off the coast. From my chair on Star Island I drew Appledore Island.

My sketch of the water, waves, rocks, seaweed, and wildflowers is complete. I included two rowboats that can be rented.

This sprawling, late 1800s industrial building on Islington Street in the West End was once the shoe button capital of the world. After high button shoes went out, the company made mattress buttons, golf tees, and WWII gas masks. Since 1986 or so, the building has provided studio spaces for artists. I drew the narrow end of the solid brick structure.

In a small, low, brick structure across the railroad tracks from
the Button Factory, I found this open door to a boat repair shop.
The red and blue boat that was being repainted and repaired had
been built there twenty years before.

It's a study in theme and variation to draw various street decorative elements, all made of cast iron. The two on the left are fence posts on Islington Street; the one on the right is a flower urn on Chestnut Street.

This weathervane on Ceres Street is at eye level and easy to
see closely.

The hand sign is on the sidewalk in front of a clothing store
on Congress Street. It is rusty and looks old fashioned, but
I am guessing that it was made to look that way. It is painted,
and the fingers are formed by just bending the thin metal.

The yellow and green trimmed wooden building sits atop a hill on Marcy Street in the South End. The double tiered cupola can be seen for blocks. Originally the South Ward Meeting House, built in 1866, it has had many uses: a site for the celebration of the Emancipation Proclamation, a school, meeting hall, voting place, children's museum, and now the home of Portsmouth Public Media.

The repeated roof lines spoke to me on quiet Mechanic Street in the South End. The left has grey-blue painted clapboards, while the warehouse on the right is faced with weather-worn cedar shingles.

The view of the buildings on Mechanic Street from Peirce Island is an iconic one. It must be, as I met lots of artists with their easels, each making her own vision of the lovely scene in the South End. I was the only sketchpad artist there.

The South End is now is a residential area for the most part. This little fenced yard between the houses on Mechanic Street stopped my gaze. Many of the homes have colorfully painted exteriors, as was fashionable when they were built.

The sidewalks of Portsmouth are dotted with bloom-filled containers,
set out to get the sun. And for people to enjoy as they pass by.

The hand painted jardiniere sits on a side street in the South End.
The square one is on Market Street.

A lush blue hydrangea grows in the sun just behind a small, wrought iron fence. Some houses are lucky enough to have small gardens near the street. And the colorful plants and flowers are so carefully tended. They slowed my feet right down.

Pattern, repetition, variation, and color stopped my feet on Mechanic Street. Then I became intrigued with it all, studying exactly how the kayaks are stored while awaiting a rental customer. While drawing, I was free to ponder on what exciting adventures each boat has had.

The fence at Geno's Chowder and Sandwich Shop on Mechanic Street is a weathered grey from the salt air. The lobster buoys and cork floats are all faded from use and from the sun. The scene is within sight of several lobster boats at their moorings, done for the day.

The porch view from Geno's prompted a lingering sketch at dessert time. It was a pleasing but complex scene of low tide, lobsters boats, grey weathered sheds, and flags. The drawbridge is off to the left, and the bridge to Peirce Island is to the right. The awning makes a colorful frame.

One day I drew the most colorful boats in Little Harbor, just past the Peirce Island bridge. The boats shifted around in the moving tidal river, making drawing even more challenging.

A closed garden gate always intrigues. The yellow green of the shrubbery contrasts nicely with the cool teal blue of the painted wood. The straight lines of the boards are having a little conversation with the curved trunks of the old guarding bushes. The sun is shining on the brick behind the gate, creating the glowing orange strip. The gate is in the South End, somewhere.

A curvy wrought iron gate on Mechanic Street is backlit with yellow sunshine. Orange trumpet flowers dangle enticingly over the wooden fence. The gate designer was inspired by the shapes of a growing stem and tendrils. An anchor in deep shadow escaped my notice for quite a while.

The buildings on Marcy Street in the South End are almost all wooden clapboarded structures, many brightly painted. These two old structures have similar windows, different rooflines, and sit at slightly different angles to the street. And both businesses are loved by area folks, who can walk there for fresh seafood, bread, cheese, and wine. Most of life's necessities really.

An island for one, or one house anyway, Round Island is on Little
Harbor in the South End. The fog shrouded the land in the distance.
A few heaps of seaweed in the foreground tell me I drew this at
low tide.

The Sheafe Warehouse was moved to its present location in Prescott Park after the Prescott sisters bought the land near the river in 1932. When it was originally built in the early 1700s, it was close by the Peirce Island Bridge at the right.

Prescott Park, on the banks of the Piscataqua River, is a large public space. There's a cooling fountain under tall shade trees, a beloved outdoor summer theater, benches, views of Maine, and a walled garden. These labeled flower beds are a part of a teaching garden.

The proportions of this yellow shingled boathouse on Mechanic Street appealed to me. In the background is the Piscataqua River, in the South End.

Yellow in the sun, purple in the shade, green arch, teal door, granite steps. This spot on Mechanic Street has all the ingredients, simple though they may be, to slow my step. And to give a little sigh in appreciation.

Observation of details automatically leads to theme and variation.
How many of these decorative elements are still with us today?
Most of them. The doors are located on Mechanic Street, Islington
Street, Hancock Street, and Pleasant Street.

The doorway on the Moffatt-Ladd House on Market Street is one
of the grandest in the city. It runs right up from ground level to
the roof. The decorative elements and the house itself are all
constructed of wood. Lumber was and is plentiful in New Hampshire.
In other areas, like England, these columns, rosettes, dentil molding,
and the like may well have been carved of stone.

This old, carefully pruned and tended tree lives in a walled garden on Marcy Street, within Prescott Park. A fence of white painted wood and iron makes a nice visual contrast to the very sinuous curved lines of the tree.

Long shadows of an autumn day were exaggerating the shapes of doorways and lights. The repeated green glass bottles on the inside, matched with the lineup of the small pumpkins on the outside of the arch. This called to me. Even more telling of a moment in time was the white padded envelope leaning against the door. Howard Street, South End.

This deeply purple house on Islington Street is eye catching. I believe it used to be white or maybe pale blue. The scalloped white wood edging trim alone says 'look at me'.

The purple house on Washington Street in the South End is more of
a grey-purple. The doorway is modest with its flattened columns, but
the blooming hollyhock is extra grand.

A sale was going on this day, as indicated by the comfortable-looking
upholstered chair on the narrow front lawn. It nearly did lure me in.

The white, wooden, ornate steeple of the North Church dominates the Market Square area. By making a change in my art materials and technique, the drawing has a looser, more atmospheric feel.

And another view of Market Street looking uphill towards Market Square. The repeated shapes of the streetlights glowing at dusk compelled me to draw.

I started my book project in January, coming over to Portsmouth whenever the weather promised to be above the freezing mark. Snow transforms the roads and the roofs in this major intersection of Pleasant Street and Marcy Street in the South End.

Turning to the right, look up Marcy Street. The traffic is usually slow in the South End.

The lantern on South Mill Street casts off spooky shapes
at the end of day.

The Point of Graves Burial Ground on the corner of Mechanic Street and Marcy Street presents a stark visual image in winter's snow. The carved slate markers have pretty flowers and vines, as well as grim skulls with wings. The people who carved gravestones were proud of their skills and usually had personal stylistic motifs.

I started the drawing outside, and then finished the piece while sitting indoors in the warm café. The skaters are gliding past the buildings at Strawbery Banke on the Labrie Family Skate at Puddle Dock Pond.

The winter sunset silhouetted the North Church Steeple. With pencil and watercolor, I did my best to record the inspiring view of Portsmouth, the small city by the sea.

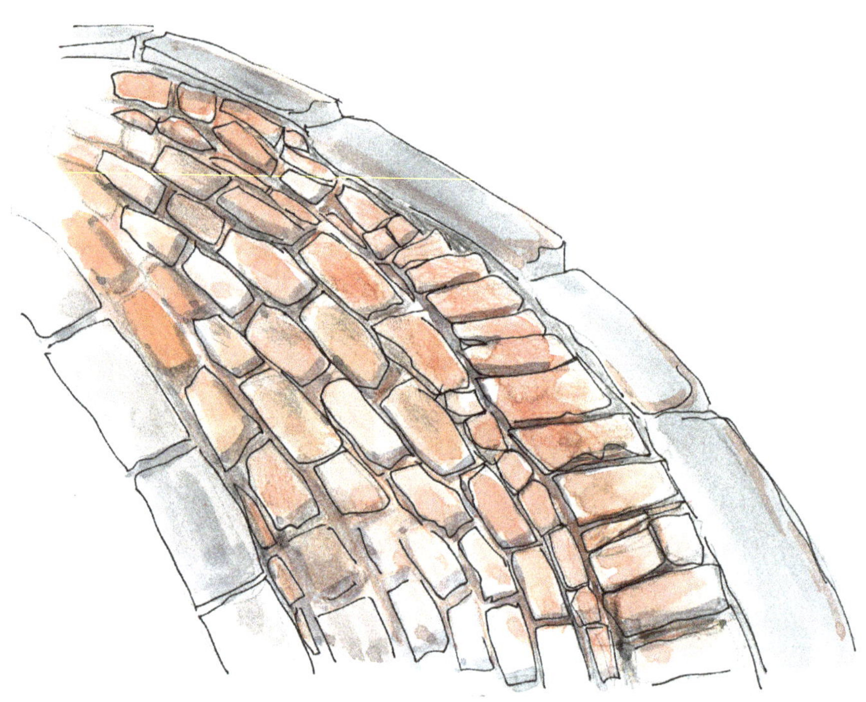

All the images were drawn on site from direct observation.
The materials I used are: pencil, pen, charcoal, water-soluble
colored pencils, water-soluble graphite pencils, water-soluble
crayons, and watercolors.

If you would like to see more of my travel sketches, find me
at www.colorfuljourney.art.